Too Shy to Say Hi

**Books for Kids From the
American Psychological Association**

Magination Press is a registered trademark of the American Psychological Association. Order books at maginationpress.org, or call 1-800-374-2721.

Book design by Rachel Ross
Printed by Phoenix Color, Hagerstown, MD

Library of Congress Cataloging-in-Publication Data
Names: Anderson, Shannon, 1972- author. | Nakata, Hiroe, illustrator.
Title: Too shy to say hi / by Shannon Anderson ; illustrated by Hiroe Nakata.
Description: Washington : Magination Press, 2021. | Summary: Determined not to let another school day pass without trying to make a friend, Shelli takes small steps toward overcoming her shyness. Includes a note about shyness.
Identifiers: LCCN 2020029931 (print) | LCCN 2020029932 (ebook) | ISBN 9781433831584 (hardcover) | ISBN 9781433835148 (ebook)
Subjects: CYAC: Bashfulness—Fiction. | Friendship—Fiction. | First day of school—Fiction. | Schools—Fiction.
Classification: LCC PZ7.1.A5314 Too 2021 (print) | LCC PZ7.1.A5314 (ebook) | DDC [E]—dc23
LC record available at https://lccn.loc.gov/2020029931
LC ebook record available at https://lccn.loc.gov/2020029932

Manufactured in the United States of America
10 9 8 7 6 5 4 3 2 1

Too Shy to Say Hi

By **Shannon Anderson**
Illustrated by **Hiroe Nakata**

Magination Press • Washington, DC
American Psychological Association

My dog and I walk every day,
just the two of us.
We pass some kids out playing ball—

"Let's *GO*, Barnabus."

"Come and join us, Shelli!"

I hear one of them say...

I give a tiny smile, but keep going on my way.

My brave dog always wants to sniff everyone in sight.

He tugs at me...
            but I tug back...
and pull with all my might.

Barnabus has no trouble
meeting friends hairless or furry.
He goes right up and greets them,
without a single worry.

We find a quiet spot at last,
beneath a shady tree.
A neighbor runs past with her dog.
I *think* she waved at me.

What if I imagined it?
Should I tell her "hi?"

I can hardly say a word
whenever I feel shy.

At home my parrot flaps her wings in her friendly way.

"Hi hiiiiii! HELLO!"

Lulu squawks.

"Easy for *you* to say."

The only one who understands
eyes me from his cave.

He loves his little hideaway:

Stan the Not-So-Brave.

I'm lucky to have three buddies
with feathers, fins, and fur.
I thought these friends would be enough...
now I'm not so sure.

When I am back at school next week
I want to give it a go!
Will someone want to play with me?
There's only one way to know.

I stare at myself in the mirror.
I wave and just say hi.
It feels a little silly,
but I know I want to try.

In the morning, I decide:
Today will be the day!
I'm going to find the courage
to be friendly in small ways.

I really want to be brave at school,
but I'm having serious doubts.
I know it won't feel good at all
if I give up and chicken out.

I've been scared for long enough, and I really want some friends. So, I'm going to talk to *someone* before another school day ends.

As the kids come into class,
I look towards Lupita's spot.

I make myself take a step,
but my stomach is in knots.

I take a single huge, deep breath.
This is the moment that I feared.

I turn the color of ketchup.
What if she thinks I'm weird?

Then I open my mouth to speak,
like I practiced in the mirror.

I manage to say the words,

"Is anyone sitting here?"

Lupita looks up and smiles.
"Hi, Shelli! Have a seat!"

I say thanks, put down my things,
and breathe a sigh of relief.

WOW! That really worked!
It wasn't SO hard, I guess.
I think I could do it again,
and worry a little bit less.

Soon it'll be time for recess.
No swinging alone again!
This might be the scariest part
of my mission to make a friend.

Things have gone well so far,
but what am I going to say?

I tap Lupita's shoulder and ask,

"At recess... do you want to play?"

"Sure!
Do you want to shoot baskets?
Or jump rope, or play baseball?"

It *all* sounds good to me.
This is the very best day of all.

I don't need to worry
and wonder.
I don't have to feel
so scared.

I can smile and say, **"Hello!"**
without having a speech prepared.

Look out world—it's Shelli!
Today went really well.

I know I have a ways to go,
but I'm peeking out of my shell!

Reader's Note

In *Too Shy to Say Hi*, Shelli experiences fear and anxiety about participating in everyday social situations, like playing with neighborhood kids and attending school. These feelings preoccupy her thoughts and stop her from joining in on activities that she would certainly enjoy. This pattern of feelings and behaviors can best be described as social anxiety. If your child struggles with feelings of shyness or social anxiety, there are many steps you can take to help them manage their anxiety.

Shyness or Social Anxiety?

Many children are naturally shy. Psychologists would say that for these children, shyness is a part of their temperament: the personality traits that determine the unique way in which they interact with the world. Most shy children "warm up" after becoming familiar with a person or situation. However, sometimes shyness becomes so extreme that it interferes with a person's social development, causing significant distress. *Social anxiety* is a term used to describe when a person avoids everyday social activities because they're worried about being judged, or they fear behaving in ways that might bring about embarrassment. Usually people with social anxiety don't have any trouble interacting with family members and close friends, but the idea of meeting new people, speaking in public, or unfamiliar situations can put their anxiety symptoms into high gear.

Fight-or-Flight

We all feel anxious or scared at times. In fact, feeling anxious can be helpful in certain situations. Our bodies and brains are hardwired to feel anxious and respond to these feelings as part of our *fight-or-flight* response, which prepares us to act quickly when we sense that danger is near. When our brains sense danger, they release adrenaline and other chemicals that cause all kinds of bodily reactions, like quickened heartbeats and rapid breathing, dilated pupils, sweating, even goosebumps! These are all part of our fight-or flight response, warning us to get ready, because we might be in danger!

Evolutionarily speaking, the fight-or-flight response was helpful because it warned early humans to react when predators were near. The dangerous presence would cause an immediate change in the person's body chemistry, allowing them to either more capably fight off the predator or have the energy to escape.

Today, the fight-or-flight response continues to keep us safe from harm—just different types of harm than our early human ancestors faced. If our bodies didn't alert us to danger by feeling fear, we wouldn't survive for very long; we'd be walking into oncoming traffic, stepping into open elevator shafts, and eating spoiled food without a second thought. Fear serves a pretty useful purpose in preventing us from doing some incredibly dangerous things!

But what about when the danger isn't real? When someone has social anxiety, or any type of anxiety problem for that matter, they feel anxious in situations in which there is no real danger at all. Their fight-or-flight response gets activated too frequently, too powerfully, and in situations where it isn't actually necessary. The body's reactions (increased heartbeat, sweating, rapid breathing) can be quite intense and so the person experiences the situation as if they were really in physical danger and their mind goes through all the associated emotions like fear and anxiety.

How Does Social Anxiety Affect Daily Life?

Social anxiety disorder is a common mental health diagnosis in childhood, with the typical age of onset between 8 and 15 years old. People with social anxiety have fears regarding their social performance. They tend to be highly self-conscious and have an extreme fear of being judged by others—and school is an extremely social time for most kids! Kids spend several hours at school each weekday, interacting with peers and teachers. Like Shelli in the book, social anxiety can keep kids from participating in everyday school and extracurricular activities, because they're too worried about what others think of them. Recess, lunch, and other "unstructured" times are often the worst for children with social anxiety because there is the most opportunity for social rejection. While in class, kids will often avoid raising their hands, even when they know the answers to teachers' questions, which can keep them from getting the most benefit out of academic instruction. It can also limit their access to positive reinforcement from teachers for answering questions correctly, and potentially mask areas of weakness in which they may need additional teacher help.

How to Help Your Child

Distinguishing between shyness and more debilitating social anxiety can be difficult. Regardless of whether you believe your child is naturally shy or experiencing social anxiety, you may want some tips to help them become more confident and comfortable interacting with others. The following are some ideas for school-aged children:

* **Arrange playdates with a single, trusted friend.** If the playdate is at the friend's house, your child may be more comfortable initially if you go along.

* **Practice public speaking at home.** Do this before any type of class presentation, show-and-tell, beginning of school introductions, etc. The more comfortable your child gets speaking in front of people, the better.

* **Do not compare your child to a less shy sibling or peer.** Instead, reinforce them for small improvements or strides they take in overcoming shyness (like making eye contact, ordering at a restaurant, etc.).

* **Prepare your child for public gatherings.** Give your child a "heads up" before social events, so they can mentally prepare. Remind them that they are safe and you will be close by if they need you.

* **Encourage a social extra-curricular.** Help your child choose one extra-curricular activity that has a social component that interests them. This can be a natural way for your child to practice their social skills in an activity of interest to them.

* **Encourage relaxation strategies.** Strategies such as deep breathing, meditation, and progressive muscle relaxation have been shown to help reduce intense physical symptoms in the moment so individuals can focus on using coping strategies.

* **Use cognitive reframing.** People with social anxiety tend to catastrophize situations, thinking in worst case scenarios. Help your child to reframe these unhelpful thoughts with more helpful ones. For instance, try replacing the negative thought "everyone will think I'm stupid if I answer the question wrong," with "everyone gets questions wrong sometimes, I don't think the other kids are stupid when they answer wrong, so why would they think that about me?"

* **Seek professional help.** If you believe that your child's anxiety is negatively affecting their ability to attend school, interact with peers, or some other area of functioning, do not hesitate to seek help from a trained mental health professional. Social anxiety disorder is a very treatable condition, and with the help of a therapist, kids can learn skills to cope with their anxiety.

Overcoming social anxiety takes hard work, lots of practice, and the courage to face one's fears and take part in new experiences. You can help your child build skills to manage their social anxiety and take baby steps toward overcoming their shyness, just like Shelli did!

Elizabeth McCallum, PhD, is an associate professor in the school psychology program at Duquesne University, as well as a Pennsylvania certified school psychologist. She is the author of many scholarly journal articles and book chapters on topics including academic and behavioral interventions for children and adolescents.

Shannon Anderson has taught first grade through college level and loves to write books for children and teachers. In 2019, Shannon was named one of the Top 10 Teachers who inspired *The Today Show*. She was named the JC Runyon Person of the Year for her work writing and speaking about social and emotional issues for kids. She lives in Indiana.

Visit shannonisteaching.com
[f] @AuthorShannonAnderson
[t] @ShannonTeaches

Hiroe Nakata grew up in Japan, encouraged in her drawing by her grandfather, a painter, and graduated from the Parsons School of Design. Illustrations from her first children's books were chosen for a Society of Illustrators Annual Exhibition. She lives in Tokyo, Japan.

[○] @HiroeNakata

Magination Press is the children's book imprint of the American Psychological Association. APA works to advance psychology as a science and profession and as a means of promoting health and human welfare. Magination Press books reach young readers and their parents and caregivers to make navigating life's challenges a little easier. It's the combined power of psychology and literature that makes a Magination Press book special.

Visit maginationpress.org
[f][t][○][p] @MaginationPress